SEVERE WEATHER

DROUGHTS

BY MEGAN GENDELL

WWW.APEXEDITIONS.COM

Copyright © 2023 by Apex Editions, Mendota Heights, MN 55120. All rights reserved. No part of this book may be reproduced or utilized in any form or by any means without written permission from the publisher.

Apex is distributed by North Star Editions:
sales@northstareditions.com | 888-417-0195

Produced for Apex by Red Line Editorial.

Photographs ©: Shutterstock Images, cover, 1, 6, 8–9, 10–11, 12–13, 13, 14–15, 18, 19, 22–23, 24–25, 27, 29; iStockphoto, 4–5, 7, 9, 16–17, 20–21

Library of Congress Control Number: 2022901432

ISBN
978-1-63738-301-8 (hardcover)
978-1-63738-337-7 (paperback)
978-1-63738-406-0 (ebook pdf)
978-1-63738-373-5 (hosted ebook)

Printed in the United States of America
Mankato, MN
082022

NOTE TO PARENTS AND EDUCATORS

Apex books are designed to build literacy skills in striving readers. Exciting, high-interest content attracts and holds readers' attention. The text is carefully leveled to allow students to achieve success quickly. Additional features, such as bolded glossary words for difficult terms, help build comprehension.

CHAPTER 1
DRY AS DUST 4

CHAPTER 2
CAUSES AND EFFECTS 10

CHAPTER 3
DANGEROUS DROUGHTS 16

CHAPTER 4
SAVING WATER 22

COMPREHENSION QUESTIONS • 28
GLOSSARY • 30
TO LEARN MORE • 31
ABOUT THE AUTHOR • 31
INDEX • 32

CHAPTER 1

DRY AS DUST

It has not rained in months. The sun beats down. Leaves turn brown and die. There is no more **moisture** in the soil.

Droughts can cause cracks to appear in the dry ground.

A lightning strike during a drought can start a dangerous wildfire.

A thunderstorm rolls in. Lightning strikes. A dry tree catches fire. Fire spreads across the dead grass.

During a drought, wildfires can quickly get out of hand. Forests can burn for weeks.

FAST FACT

Droughts make wildfires more likely. Dry plants catch fire easily.

Soon, the rain comes. It puts out the fire. But the rain falls too fast. The soil can't soak it up. After the storm, the soil dries up again. The drought continues.

If heavy rain comes after a drought, land can flood.

Tree rings can show the health and age of a tree.

STUDYING TREES

Scientists study tree rings to learn about past droughts. Tree rings are thinner during dry years. Scientists can see how often droughts have happened.

CHAPTER 2

CAUSES AND EFFECTS

A drought happens when an area gets less rain than normal. Without enough **precipitation**, plants die. There is less food for animals and people.

Many plants that people grow for food need lots of water. A drought can kill them.

FAST FACT

Wind can blow dry dirt into the air during a drought. This creates a dust storm.

Droughts also cause lakes and rivers to dry up. Water supplies may run out.

If streams and rivers dry up, some people may not have water to drink.

In a drought, less grass grows. Animals such as cows may run out of food.

Dry weather may last for weeks or years before people know a drought is happening. Most droughts end slowly, too. Enough water must soak back into the ground.

It's normal for deserts to go many days without rain. But droughts can still take place there. They just take longer to happen.

STREAMS OF AIR

Miles high in the sky, fast winds blow in a path called the jet stream. This path can change. When that happens, rain can stop coming to some places. Droughts can happen there.

CHAPTER 3

DANGEROUS DROUGHTS

Droughts can be dangerous. Long ago, ancient Egypt had a serious drought. Many people who built the **pyramids** died.

Egyptians built the pyramids more than 4,000 years ago.

In the 1930s, many people had to leave their homes after a drought killed their crops.

A bad drought hit a large part of the United States in the 1930s. This event was called the Dust Bowl. Many **crops** died. People had little food.

Huge dust storms during the Dust Bowl killed many people and animals.

FAST FACT
The drought in the Dust Bowl lasted about 10 years.

Syria had a drought from 2006 to 2010. Farmers could not grow enough food. Many people faced **famine**.

Many people in Syria raise livestock. The bad drought there killed many animals.

CHANGING CLIMATE

Climate change has made many places hotter and drier. This can cause droughts. A drought hit Madagascar in 2017. It was the area's worst drought in 35 years. An even worse drought came in 2021.

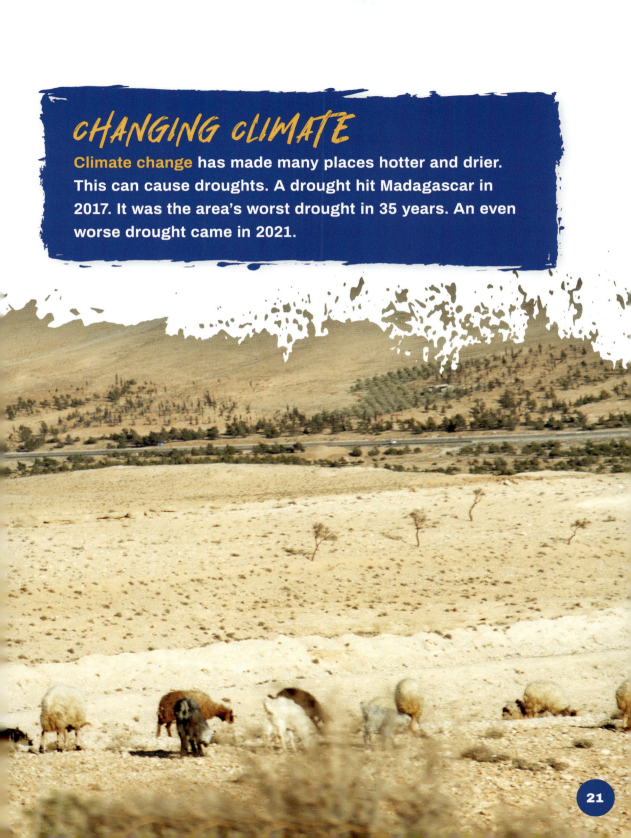

CHAPTER 4

SAVING WATER

Droughts cannot be **prevented**. But people can plan for them. For example, cities can collect water when it rains. This water can be used during droughts.

Some places collect rainwater in large tanks. They save the water to use later.

Black-eyed peas don't need much water to grow.

Using less water helps, too. Farmers can plant crops that don't need as much water. These crops are better at surviving droughts. They also save more water for drinking.

FAST FACT

People can **recycle** water, too. They collect dirty water and clean it.

As climate change continues, droughts may become more common. People are finding new ways to make sure dry areas have enough water.

DRINKING THE OCEAN

Earth's oceans have lots of water. But that water is too salty for people. However, people can use machines to remove the salt. That makes the water safe to drink.

Desalination plants turn salt water into fresh water that people can drink.

COMPREHENSION QUESTIONS

Write your answers on a separate piece of paper.

1. Write a few sentences describing some of the problems a drought can cause.

2. Do you think it is worse to have too much rain or not enough rain? Why?

3. What is the definition of a drought?
   - A. when an area gets more rain than normal
   - B. when an area gets less rain than normal
   - C. when an area gets no rain for six days

4. Why may it take a long time to realize a drought is happening?
   - A. because people do not pay attention
   - B. because people like dry weather
   - C. because droughts happen slowly over time

5. What does **soak** mean in this book?

But the rain falls too fast. The soil can't soak it up.

    A. to take in water
    B. to send out water
    C. to shake back and forth

6. What does **surviving** mean in this book?

Farmers can plant crops that don't need as much water. These crops are better at surviving droughts.

    A. causing
    B. dying from
    C. living through

Answer key on page 32.

29

GLOSSARY

climate change
A dangerous long-term change in Earth's temperature and weather patterns.

crops
Plants that people grow for food.

famine
An extreme lack of food over a long period of time.

moisture
Water in very small drops.

precipitation
Water that falls to the ground as rain, sleet, hail, or snow.

prevented
Kept from happening.

pyramids
Giant buildings made by the ancient Egyptians. Pyramids have four slanted sides that meet in a point.

recycle
To use something again.

BOOKS

Gagliardi, Sue. *East African Drought of 2011*. Lake Elmo, MN: Focus Readers, 2020.

Pettiford, Rebecca. *Droughts*. Minneapolis: Bellwether Media, 2020.

Tomecek, Steve. *All About Heat Waves and Droughts*. New York: Children's Press, 2021.

ONLINE RESOURCES

Visit **www.apexeditions.com** to find links and resources related to this title.

ABOUT THE AUTHOR

Megan Gendell is a writer and editor. She lives in Vermont. She loves big thunderstorms.

INDEX

A
animals, 10

C
climate change, 21, 26
crops, 18, 25

D
Dust Bowl, 18–19

E
Egypt, 16

F
farmers, 20, 25
fire, 6–8
food, 10, 18, 20

M
moisture, 4

P
plants, 7, 10

R
rain, 4, 8, 10, 15, 22

S
soil, 4, 8
Syria, 20

T
tree rings, 8

W
water, 12, 14, 22, 25, 26
wind, 12, 15

ANSWER KEY:
1. Answers will vary; 2. Answers will vary; 3. B; 4. C; 5. A; 6. C